Dr. Jennifer Chambers is a graduate of Eastern Kentucky University where she earned her BS in Elementary Education, MAEd as a Reading/Writing Specialist, Rank 1, and EdD in Educational Leadership and Policy Studies. Currently, Dr. Chambers serves as the Director of the Literacy Specialist Program and a Professor of Literacy at the University of the Cumberlands in Williamsburg, KY. Prior to her career in higher education, she served as an elementary classroom teacher for fifteen years.

Macie Meets
Her New Teacher

Jennifer R. Chambers

AUSTIN MACAULEY PUBLISHERS™
LONDON • CAMBRIDGE • NEW YORK • SHARJAH

Copyright © Jennifer R. Chambers (2019)

Ordering Information:
Quantity sales: special discounts are available on quantity purchases by corporations, associations, and others. For details, contact the publisher at the address below.

R. Chambers, Jennifer
Macie Meets Her New Teacher

ISBN 9781643788173 (Paperback)
ISBN 9781643788180 (Hardback)
ISBN 9781645365273 (ePub e-book)

Library of Congress Control No: 2019910685

The main category of the book — JUVENILE FICTION / Social Themes / New Experience
www.austinmacauley.com/us

First Published (2019)
Austin Macauley Publishers LLC
40 Wall Street, 28th Floor
New York, NY 10005
USA

mail-usa@austinmacauley.com
+1 (646) 5125767

I would like to dedicate this book to my sweet, smart, and sassy first born granddaughter, Macie Renee. May you love school and learning as much as your GG always has. I can't wait to watch you continue to grow and see what amazing things the future has in store for you!

I would like to thank my family, especially my husband, who has always encouraged me and stood beside me no matter what. I would not be where I am today without your continuous love and support.

It was Macie's first day at her new school. She was so excited to make new friends, learn lots of new things, and most of all, meet her new teacher. She woke up very early because she was so excited (and a little nervous). Her mommy made her favorite breakfast — strawberries, yogurt, and chocolate milk.

After Macie finished eating, it was time to get dressed. She wore her favorite yellow dress and yellow hairband with a bow. She was ready to start her day! Macie's mommy, daddy, and little sister, Haley, all kissed her goodbye, and she was on her way.

Macie got on the bus and took her seat up front. She noticed a nice-looking lady sitting in the seat next to her. She asked the lady,
"Are you my new teacher?"
The nice lady smiled and replied, "No, I am the bus monitor. I help load and unload students and make sure everyone is well-behaved.
I also help make sure that you are safe on the school bus."

When Macie arrived at school, the bus monitor helped her off the bus, and Macie walked into the building. There was a lady standing at the door with a big smile, greeting all the students as they entered the school. Macie just knew this had to be her teacher. She excitedly asked, "Are you my new teacher?"

The lady smiled at Macie and replied, "No, I am the school counselor. My job is to make sure you have all the things you need and I am here if you ever need to talk to anyone."

Macie liked the counselor and the idea that she could go talk to her if she ever needed anything.

The counselor directed students to the cafeteria where breakfast was being served. Macie had already eaten at home, but they were having pancakes with syrup today, so she decided it would be okay to eat again.

She asked the lady serving the pancakes, "Are you my new teacher?"
The lady replied, "No, I am a cafeteria worker.
I help cook and serve students food for breakfast and lunch."
Macie enjoyed her pancakes and looked forward to going back for lunch to
see what the nice lady would be serving them.

As Macie was leaving the cafeteria, she noticed a gentleman helping some students clean up a spill.
She thought to herself that this was very nice, so she walked over and asked the man, "Are you my new teacher?"
The man smiled and replied, "No, I am the custodian. I spend my days cleaning and making sure the school is secure for you and all the other students."
Macie thought to herself that this was a very important job. She thanked the man and left the cafeteria to continue her search for her new teacher.

As Macie was walking down the hallway, she saw a man and a lady standing near the office talking. She thought for sure one of these people would be her teacher. She stopped and said,
"Excuse me. Are one of you my new teacher?"
The man and lady stopped talking and the man said, "No, I am the principal and this is the school secretary. I am the leader of the school.

It is my responsibility to supervise all the students and teachers. Ms. Souder —the secretary — helps me by answering important phone calls, communicating with parents and community members, and keeping up with what is going on at school on a day to day basis."

Macie said, "Wow! That sounds like a lot."

They both laughed and the principal offered to walk Macie to her classroom.

As they were walking down the hall, Macie admired all of the decorated
doors of different classrooms.
She couldn't wait to see what hers looked like.

Finally, the principal stopped at a door that had a picture of a big box of crayons on it, and all around the box were different colored crayons with names on them.
Macie found her name on a yellow crayon.
She excitedly said, "There's my name! Yellow is my favorite color!"

They walked in the door and Macie saw a lady standing in the front of the room writing something on the board. She ran over and asked, "Are you my new teacher?"

The lady stopped writing and looked at Macie and said, "Yes, I am!"
Finally, Macie had found her new teacher.

She had an amazing first day and couldn't wait to go home and tell her family about all the new people she had met, her new classroom, and most of all — her new teacher.